BLACKBERRY FARM

ERNEST OWL STARTS A SCHOOL

Jane Pilgrim

This edition first published in the United Kingdom in 1999 by
Brockhampton Press
20 Bloomsbury Street
London WC1B 3QA
a member of the Hodder Headline PLC Group

© Text copyright MCMLII by Jane Pilgrim
© Illustrations copyright MCMLII by Hodder & Stoughton Ltd

Designed and Produced for Brockhampton Press by
Open Door Limited
80 High Street, Colsterworth, Lincolnshire, NG33 5JA

Illustrator: F. Stocks May
Colour separation: GA Graphics Stamford

Title: BLACKBERRY FARM, Ernest Owl Starts a School
ISBN: 1-84186-006-9

ERNEST OWL STARTS A SCHOOL

Jane Pilgrim

Illustrated by F. Stocks May

BROCKHAMPTON PRESS

It was a very good idea. Ernest Owl thought of it one night as he sat on a branch of his old oak tree and watched the moon shining down on Blackberry Farm. "I will start a school," he hooted softly to himself. "and all the little ones at the farm shall come to me, and I will teach them, and everyone will be pleased." So he began to make a list.

First of all there were
Mrs Nibble's three little bunnies,
Rosy, Posy and Christopher. They
were in bed with measles, but they
would soon be better.

Then there was little Martha the
Lamb, and Mother Hen's naughty
little chick Mary. "Mother Hen will
be very glad," Ernest Owl thought,
"because I know she wants to be
alone to lay some more eggs."

That made five altogether, and then Ernest Owl decided to ask George the Kitten as well. He found him one evening waiting by the farmhouse door for his supper. "If I start a school, George," he began solemnly, "will you come? I shall want you to be head boy, and see that the others are good." George thought that would be fun, so he said: "Yes, Ernest Owl, I will come."

The next thing to do was to find a place for the school, and Ernest Owl chose a little shed next to the stable where Emily the Goat lived. "That will be very useful," he told himself, "because Emily can provide milk for the little ones in the morning." And when he asked Emily, she said she would be very pleased to do it.

Little Martha the Lamb was very excited when she heard that she was to go to school. "When can I come, Ernest Owl?" she bleated. "Can I come to-morrow?" But Ernest said that the school would not start until he had asked Lucy Mouse to clean the shed for them.

The next day Lucy Mouse started work. She swept and she dusted and she tidied, and by the evening everything was spotless. Ernest was delighted, and George the Kitten helped to arrange some old boxes as tables and some plant-pots as stools ready for the lessons.

At nine o'clock the next morning
Ernest Owl opened the door of his
school and took his place at the
teacher's table and waited.

First of all Mrs Nibble hurried
up with her three little bunnies,
and they sat in the front because
they were the youngest. Then
Mother Hen bustled in with Little
Mary, and behind her came
Martha the Lamb. They sat in the
next row. Last of all, but very
important, came George the
Kitten, and he sat all by himself at
the back.

Ernest Owl put on a large pair of spectacles and looked down at them. Then he took up a large piece of paper and a large pencil. "Good morning, everybody," he said. "Are you all here?" And they all said: "Yes, Ernest Owl." And he ticked off their names on his list.

After that they began their work.
The bunnies learnt to write R for
Rosy, P for Posy and C for
Christopher. Mary Hen was taught
to count up marbles so that she
could tell how many eggs her
mother had laid. George and Little
Martha drew pictures of
Blackberry Farm.

At eleven o'clock Ernest Owl
rang a little bell. "You have
worked very hard," he hooted.
"Now we shall stop for a little
while. Emily the Goat has put
some milk for you all outside. Go
and find it."

And outside on an old bench they found six mugs of milk. One for each of them. When they had drunk their milk, Ernest Owl rang the bell again, and they all went back into the school. "Now you shall sing and dance until it is time to go home," he told them. So they all played "Ring-a-ring o' Roses" and sang Nursery Rhymes until it was time to stop.

Then Ernest Owl opened the
door for them to go home. "Good-
bye," he said. "You have all been
very good. Come again to-morrow
at the same time." So they all said
good-bye, and George the Kitten
said: "I think Ernest Owl is very
clever. I'm going to like having a
school at Blackberry Farm." And
they all agreed with him.